Dear Parent:

Congratulations! Your child is taking the first steps on an exciting journey. The destination? Independent reading!

STEP INTO READING® will help your child get there. The program offers books at five levels that accompany children from their first attempts at reading to reading success. Each step includes fun stories, fiction and nonfiction, and colorful art. There are also Step into Reading Sticker Books, Step into Reading Math Readers, Step into Reading Write-In Readers, Step into Reading Phonics Readers, and Step into Reading Phonics First Steps! Boxed Sets—a complete literacy program with something to interest every child.

Learning to Read, Step by Step!

Ready to Read Preschool–Kindergarten
• big type and easy words • rhyme and rhythm • picture clues
For children who know the alphabet and are eager to begin reading.

Reading with Help Preschool–Grade 1
• basic vocabulary • short sentences • simple stories
For children who recognize familiar words and sound out new words with help.

Reading on Your Own Grades 1–3
• engaging characters • easy-to-follow plots • popular topics
For children who are ready to read on their own.

Reading Paragraphs Grades 2–3
• challenging vocabulary • short paragraphs • exciting stories
For newly independent readers who read simple sentences with confidence.

Ready for Chapters Grades 2–4
• chapters • longer paragraphs • full-color art
For children who want to take the plunge into chapter books but still like colorful pictures.

STEP INTO READING® is designed to give every child a successful reading experience. The grade levels are only guides. Children can progress through the steps at their own speed, developing confidence in their reading, no matter what their grade.

Remember, a lifetime love of reading starts with a single step!

Copyright © 2004 Disney Enterprises, Inc. Based on the "Winnie the Pooh" works, by A. A. Milne and E. H. Shepard. All rights reserved under International and Pan-American Copyright Conventions. Published in the United States by Random House Children's Books, a division of Random House Inc., New York, and simultaneously in Canada by Random House of Canada Limited, Toronto, in conjunction with Disney Enterprises, Inc.
www.randomhouse.com/kids/disney

www.stepintoreading.com

Educators and librarians, for a variety of teaching tools, visit us at
www.randomhouse.com/teachers

Library of Congress Cataloging-in-Publication Data
Pooh's valentine / Based on the "Winnie the Pooh" works by A. A. Milne and E. H. Shepard
     p. cm. — (Step into reading. Step 2 book)
Summary: It is Valentine's Day in the Hundred-Acre Wood and Pooh and his friends decide to make cards to exchange with each other at a party.
ISBN: 0-7364-2264-1 (trade) — ISBN: 0-7364-8034-X (GLB)
[1. Valentines—Fiction. 2. Valentine's Day—Fiction. 3. Teddy bears—Fiction. 4. Toys—Fiction.]
I. Milne, A. A. (Alan Alexander), 1882–1956. II. Shepard, Ernest H. (Ernest Howard), 1879–1976. III. Series.

PZ7.P7754 2004 [Fic]—dc22 2003023894

Printed in the United States of America 10 9 8 7 6 5 4 3 2 1

STEP INTO READING®

STEP 2

Winnie the Pooh

Pooh's Valentine

By Isabel Gaines
Illustrated by Mark Marderosian
and Paul Lopez

Random House 🏠 New York

It was Valentine's Day in
the Hundred-Acre Wood.

Everyone was excited.

"I'm going to make
cards for all of you,"
said Pooh.

"Let's <u>all</u> make
Valentine's Day cards,"
said Rabbit.

"Good idea," said Roo.
"And we'll pass them
out at the party,"
added Kanga.

Everyone went home
to get ready
for the party.

Pooh was hungry.

He had a snack.

Then he cut out
his cards.
But Pooh made
a big mess.

"Oh, dear," said Pooh.
His cards were
sticky and dirty.

Owl made cards for
all his friends.
He put them
outside to dry.

But it started to snow.
His cards were
wet and stained.

16

Piglet made cards, too.

He went walking

with them in the woods.

But Piglet got scared.
He dropped all
his cards.

Tigger worked
on his cards.
But he could not get
them to look right.

So Tigger went
bouncing instead.

That night, the friends
had their party.
Some gave out cards.

And some only
got them.

They ate.

And they sang.

And they laughed.

Then the friends
went ice-skating.
But they saw
something odd.

Piglet's cards were
frozen in the ice.
"Thank you for
the cards," said Pooh.

Everyone started
to skate.
They made hearts
in the ice.

In the spring,
the ice melted.
The friends enjoyed
Valentine's Day again
with Piglet's cards.

Now <u>you</u> make a card
for someone special.